This book belongs to:

_____

Contents

Ladybird

Cover illustration by Trevor Parkin

Published by Ladybird Books Ltd
27 Wrights Lane London W8 5TZ
A Penguin Company
3 5 7 9 10 8 6 4

© LADYBIRD BOOKS LTD MCMXCVII

Printed in Italy

Quick as a flash

written by Marie Birkinshaw
illustrated by Jacqueline East

Anna's dad was always in a hurry,
and he hated to be kept waiting.

One morning, he was waiting
to take Anna to school as usual.
He called crossly upstairs,
"Anna! Are you coming?
I'm ready to go now."

"Yes!" Anna shouted.
"But I need a drink of water first."

"Well, come down and get one,"
said Dad. "Be as quick as a flash."

"I wish you wouldn't say that!" said Anna, when they were in the car.

"Say what?" asked Dad.

"Quick as a flash!" said Anna. "It sounds silly."

Dad just smiled.

The next day, Dad was waiting
to take Anna swimming.

"Time to go, Anna!" he said.

"But I'm not ready!" she cried.

"Well, hurry up and get ready!"
Dad called. Then he smiled
and said, "Quick as a flash!"

Anna groaned and
covered her ears with her hands.

A few days later, Dad was busy
fixing a light bulb. This time Anna
was waiting for him to take her
to a dancing class.

"Hurry up, Dad!" said Anna.

"I'm coming," said Dad.

"Well, I won't say that again!"
said Dad.

Another dog's bone

One of Aesop's fables
illustrated by Jackie Morris

One day, a hungry dog took
a bone from a shop.
He ran off with it before anyone
could stop him.

Soon he came
to a river.
He looked in it
and saw another dog
in the water.

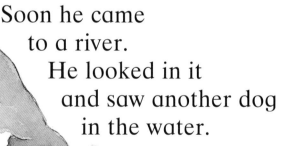

"That dog's bone looks much
juicier than mine!" thought
the hungry dog. "I'll jump in
and take it from him."

So he jumped in.
At once, the other dog
and its bone disappeared.

To make things worse, the hungry dog had also lost his own bone in the water.

He walked sadly away to look for another bone.

Moral: Beware of being greedy!

Stargazers

written by Marie Birkinshaw
illustrated by Trevor Parkin

Grandad took Sally and Tom
to see the night sky.

"Tell us a story about the stars,"
said Tom.

"All right," said Grandad.
"Here's a story that helps me
to remember their names."

Once upon a time, there was
a beautiful queen who sat on
a golden throne.
She loved to look down at
the beautiful Earth below.

Dragon

Queen

An enormous dragon was
jealous of the Queen's beauty.
He called for a big black cloud
to cover the Earth. This made
the Queen very sad.

The other stars loved the Queen
and wanted to help her. So that
night, a silver swan came
swimming through the cloud
and showed the Queen
all the shining seas
and rivers below.

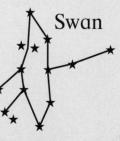

Swan

The dragon was angry and
called for more clouds.

The next night, a giant lion leapt through the clouds. He showed the Queen all the amazing animals on the Earth below.

Lion

Now the dragon became really
angry and called for more and
more clouds.
"Your friends will never get
through this," he roared.

But that night, two bears – a big bear and a little bear – raced through the clouds. They showed the Queen all the Earth's beautiful mountains. And soon she was happy again.

Great Bear and Little Bear

This time the dragon became
so angry and so jealous of the
Queen that he pushed her into
a big black hole and roared,
"Now you'll never see anything
ever again!"

25

The other stars saw what the
dragon had done.
They asked for help from the stars
at the other side of the Earth.
Together they pulled and pulled
until the Queen came out of
the big black hole...

and then together they pushed
the big bad dragon in!

"And, you know," said Grandad, "the Queen never saw that dragon again!"

"That was a lovely story," Sally said.

"Grandad, what's a shooting star?" asked Tom.

"I don't know," said Grandad. "Let's go inside and look it up in a book!"

Some stars of the northern sky

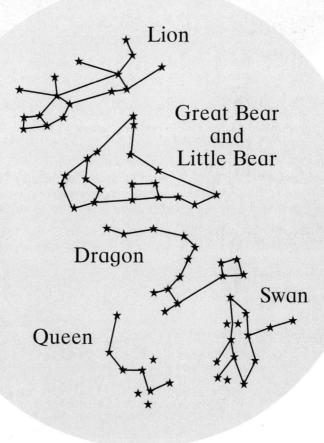

Lion

Great Bear
and
Little Bear

Dragon

Queen

Swan

Some stars of the southern sky

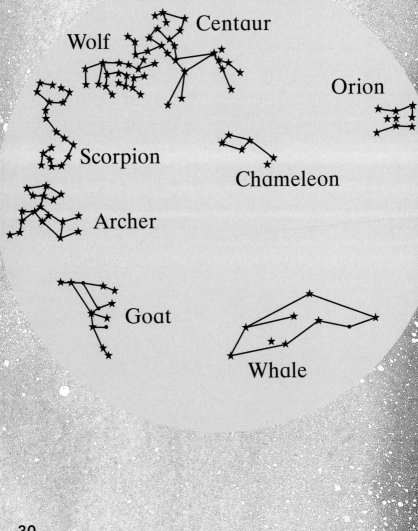

Wolf

Centaur

Orion

Scorpion

Chameleon

Archer

Goat

Whale

Did you know that?

Every star is a sun – an enormous ball of very hot gas.

The stars are millions and millions of kilometres away from Earth.
Our Sun is 150 million kilometres away.

Light from our Sun takes more than eight minutes to reach Earth.

Bunches of stars are called star clusters. One of the biggest star clusters is called The Milky Way.

When stars are new they are really hot. Really hot stars are so bright and white that they can look blue. As stars get older, they get colder and turn red.

 Shooting stars are not stars at all – they are small bits of dust that burn up as they get nearer the Earth.

Learning to read with this book

Special features

Stargazers and other stories is ideal for early independent reading. It includes:

• two long stories to build stamina.

• interesting facts for your child to read for herself.

Planned to help your child to develop her reading by:

• practising a variety of reading techniques such as recognising frequently used words on sight, being able to read words with similar spelling patterns (eg, look/book), and the use of letter-sound clues.

• using rhyme to improve memory.

• including illustrations that make reading even more enjoyable.

Read with Ladybird...

is specially designed to help your child learn to read. It will complement all the methods used in schools.

Parents took part in extensive research to ensure that **Read with Ladybird** would help your child to:

- take the first steps in reading
- improve early reading progress
- gain confidence in new-found abilities.

The research highlighted that the most important qualities in helping children to read were that:

- books should be fun – children have enough 'hard work' at school
- books should be colourful and exciting
- stories should be up to date and about everyday experiences
- repetition and rhyme are especially important in boosting a child's reading ability.

The stories and rhymes introduce the 100 words most frequently used in reading and writing.

These 100 key words actually make up half the words we use in speech and reading.

The three levels of **Read with Ladybird** consist of 22 books, taking your child from two words per page to 600-word stories.

Read with Ladybird will help your child to master the basic reading skills so vital in everyday life.

Ladybird have successfully published reading schemes and programmes for the last 50 years. Using this experience and the latest research, **Read with Ladybird** has been produced to give all children the head start they deserve.

milky

millions

minutes

mountains

names

queen

ready

remember

roared

shining

shooting

silly

sounds

star

story

swan

than

throne

together

usual

worse

For a child who is at the first reading stage – whether he or she is at school or about to start school. Uses rhyme and repetitive phrases to build sentences and introduces and emphasises important words relating to everyday childhood experiences.

Building on the reading skills taught at home and in school, this level helps your child to practise the first 100 key words. The stories help develop your child's interest in reading with structured texts while maintaining the fun of learning to read.

At this level, your child is able to practise new-found skills and move from reading out loud to independent silent reading. The longer stories and rhymes develop reading stamina and introduce different styles of writing and a variety of subjects. At the end of this level your child will have read around 1000 different words.